Noddy's Pet Chicken

HarperCollins *Children's Books*

Noddy was driving Big-Ears
through Toyland.
It was a sunny day.

Big-Ears asked Noddy to slow down.
Noddy liked to drive fast
but did as Big-Ears asked.
"I listen when people tell me
what they want," said Noddy.

Suddenly they saw a chicken
standing in the road!

"Are you lost?" asked Big-Ears.

"Maybe I should take him home,"
said Noddy.

"I will give him my favourite foods
and we'll play my favourite games."

"You funny little Noddy!"
said Big-Ears.

"I'm going to treat this chicken
very well," said Noddy.

He was so happy he sang a song:

"I'm a lucky boy,

Now I have a chicken.

He's my pet,

One I won't forget,

Now I have a chicken!"

Noddy put the chicken in the car
and began to drive very fast.
The chicken did not like riding
in the car.

"What is wrong, little chicken?"
asked Noddy.
Noddy drove more slowly.
"It will take forever
to get back to town!" he said.

Noddy drove to the Ice Cream Parlour
and bought two caramel treats.

He gave one caramel to the chicken.

"Go ahead and eat it!" said Noddy.

"It's good!"

But the chicken did not want to eat the caramel treat.

Noddy saw Dinah Doll
and asked her why his chicken
would not eat the caramel treat.

"Maybe he likes a different kind
of treat," said Dinah.

Dinah gave the chicken some corn.

The chicken loved eating the corn.

"Not everybody likes to eat
the same things," said Dinah Doll.

"Now let's climb a tree!" cried Noddy
as he ran towards the tallest tree
in Toy Town Square.

The chicken looked up at Noddy.

It did not want to climb the tree.

"Now what can we do?"

said Noddy.

Then Noddy gave the chicken
some roller skates.
But the chicken did not know
how to roller skate.

The chicken did not want to do
any of Noddy's favourite things.
"What do you want to do?" he asked.

Noddy threw a ball for the chicken.
But the chicken did not want
to play fetch.

Bumpy Dog saw the ball.

He wanted to play fetch.

He ran towards the ball

and scared the chicken.

Mr Plod saw the chicken running.

He did not like chickens.

"Noddy, take the chicken home!"

Mr Plod ordered.

Noddy asked Big-Ears for advice.

Big-Ears always knows what to do.

Big-Ears told Noddy

that chickens do not like to do

the same things that people do.

"I only thought about what I wanted

to do," said Noddy.

"We should bring the chicken
back to where we found it.
Then he might remember
where he belongs," said Big-Ears.

The chicken flew out of Noddy's car
towards a garden with a pink fence.
"This must be his home!" said Noddy.

24

"If you want the chicken to be happy,
you must let him go home,"
said Big-Ears.

"I want what is best for him.

Go home, chicken!

I will miss you!" said Noddy.

Tessie Bear was standing

in the garden.

"You found my lost chicken!" she cried.

"Thank you for bringing him back."

"Now I can feed him corn
and let him scratch the grass.
Those are his favourite things to do,"
said Tessie Bear.

"So that is what chickens like to do!"
Noddy was pleased to find out.